The Case Of The
CANDY CANE CLUE

Look for more great books in

The New Adventures of

MARY-KATE & ASHLEY™

series:

The Case Of The
CANDY CANE CLUE

by Judy Katschke

HarperEntertainment
An Imprint of HarperCollins*Publishers*

A PARACHUTE PRESS BOOK

PARACHUTE PRESS

Parachute Publishing, L.L.C.
156 Fifth Avenue
New York, NY 10010

DUALSTAR PUBLICATIONS

Dualstar Publications
c/o Thorne and Company
A Professional Law Corporation
1801 Century Park East
Los Angeles, CA 90067

HarperEntertainment

An Imprint of HarperCollins*Publishers*
10 East 53rd Street, New York, NY 10022

TOYS GALORE!

"**A**shley, check it out," I told my sister as I opened our next Christmas present. "Great-Grandma Olive just sent us a fingerprinting kit!"

Ashley sat next to me by the Christmas tree. "Cool!" she exclaimed. "Just what we always wanted!"

Ashley and I are detectives. We're ten years old and run the Olsen and Olsen Detective Agency from our attic. Great-Grandma Olive's gift would definitely come in handy when we were solving our cases.

"We could have used this kit a few days ago," Ashley said. "Right, Mary-Kate?"

"That's for sure," I agreed.

A few days ago Ashley and I went to Patty O'Leary's Christmas sleepover party. But it wasn't an ordinary popcorn and videos sleepover. It was held at Tower of Toys—the biggest toy store in town.

And there was something else that made Patty's party different. Ashley and I had to solve a mystery!

"This party is going to be awesome," Ashley said the night of the sleepover. "I've never slept in a toy store before."

"It's *got* to be an awesome party if Princess Patty is throwing it," I said. "Her parents totally spoil her."

"And today I'm glad they did!" Ashley giggled.

Ashley and I lugged our sleeping bags to

the Tower of Toys entrance. The door was decorated with colorful lights and teddy bears dressed up as elves. The store windows were filled with every toy and game we could ever imagine!

"Hey, wait for us!" our friend Samantha Kramer called.

I turned and saw Samantha rushing toward us. Our other friend, Tim Park, was right behind her. They were here for Patty's party, too.

"This store rocks!" Tim declared. "And we'll get to play with every toy in the place."

"I know," Ashley said. "I can't wait to try the latest Moon Raiders video game."

Tim pulled a crumpled piece of paper from his pocket. "I made a list of all the candy I want to eat at the Snack Shack in the store."

I laughed. Tim loved to eat more than anything!

"Well, I'm going to unroll my sleeping bag in the Margie doll section," Samantha announced.

That was no surprise. Samantha had every Margie doll ever made. Sand'n'Surf Margie, High-flying Margie, Ride 'Em Cowgirl Margie—

"Hey, look!" Samantha pointed at two people stepping out of the store: a handsome guy dressed in a Hawaiian shirt and a teenage girl with long, swingy blond hair.

"Who are *they*?" Tim asked.

"It's Margie's boyfriend and little sister," Samantha explained. "Honolulu Hal and Cricket."

"They're *dolls*?" Tim asked.

"No, silly," Ashley said. "They're real people. They're just dressed like the dolls. It's their job to walk around Tower of Toys and talk to the kids."

I smiled. They *did* look just like the dolls. But they didn't look very happy.

"Hi, guys!" Samantha called. "Are you going to be at the sleepover, too?"

"Not a chance," Hal grumbled. "We've been *fired*!"

"Tower of Toys says we're not popular anymore," Cricket wailed. "How's that for a Christmas present?"

We stared at Hal and Cricket as they walked past us. "I can't believe they were fired," I said.

"Tower of Toys won't be the same without them," Ashley said.

"Well, they'll never fire the girl who plays Margie," Samantha said. "The Margie doll has been Toy of the Year since we were in kindergarten."

We filed through the door and into the store. The place was packed with wall-to-wall games and toys. There were whole sections just for electronics, scooters and skateboards, stuffed animals, dolls, books, everything!

"This is just the main floor," Tim said. "Upstairs is the Outer Space Place, the Magic Hut, Puppet Parade, the Snack Shack, and more!"

"We know," Ashley said with a grin. "Mary-Kate and I have been here dozens of times."

But today Tower of Toys looked *extra* special. Gumdrop-covered wreaths and gigantic candy canes were hung along the walls. A huge silver Christmas tree stood in the center of the store. Its branches reached all the way up to the ceiling.

Patty peeked out from behind a giant giraffe. "There you are," she said. "Ready for the best Christmas sleepover of the century?"

"You bet!" I answered. "Is everyone here?"

Patty pointed to four girls playing tag around the Christmas tree. "Bethany, Kendra, Alexis, and Maria are here," she said. "They're all from my Sunshine Scout troop."

We waved at the girls, and they waved back.

Then I spotted a boy with spiky red hair walking around the store. He was talking into a mini–tape recorder.

"Who's he?" I asked Patty.

"That's just my cousin Melvin." Patty sighed. "I *had* to invite him."

"Cool," Tim said. "At least I won't be the only boy at this party."

I could hear Melvin barking into the recorder: "Electronic skateboard—one unit! Tubes of Freaky Foam, hot colors only—two dozen units. Mega-Monster Cycles—three units!"

"What's he doing?" Ashley whispered.

Patty rolled her eyes. "Melvin's recording his Christmas list," she said.

"And he needs *three* Mega-Monster Cycles?" I asked.

"Melvin can never have enough toys," Patty muttered. "And whatever Melvin wants, he gets, too. That's why we call him the Prince."

Ashley and I tried not to smile. We called her *Princess* Patty because Patty gets everything *she* wants.

"Hey!" Melvin said. He clicked off his recorder and pointed at Ashley and me. "Aren't you those kid detectives—the Trenchcoat Twins?"

"That's us," I said.

"Patty told me all about you," Melvin said. He picked up his tape recorder. "Super Sleuth Detective Kit—one unit. Make it two!" he ordered.

We all piled our sleeping bags around a big fake snowman standing near the electronic games. Then we went to the Christmas tree for a closer look.

"That is one serious tree," Tim said.

A woman with curly brown hair walked

into the room. She was wearing a red-and-white-striped shirt and pants. Silver jingle-bell earrings dangled from her ears. "We are going to have serious fun!" the woman announced. "I'm Candice, your party guide. But you can call me Candy. Like a candy cane!"

I liked Candy, and I liked her earrings. They jingled every time she moved her head.

"Now, if I only knew where I could find Tiny," Candy said, looking around.

"Who's Tiny?" Tim wanted to know.

"Tiny is my party assistant." Candy glanced at her watch. "And he's late," she said. "Oh, well. Let's get ready to have a blast! We'll be creating magic, playing awesome games, and dancing up a snowstorm. And at the end of the party you'll each get to take home a toy of your choice!"

"Awesome!" Kendra said.

"What are we waiting for?" Maria asked

excitedly. "Let's get this party started!"

Patty rubbed her hands together. "Show me to the toys, Candy."

Candy's earrings jingled as she shook her head back and forth. "Not yet. Before we begin, there's something I must warn you about," she said in a serious voice.

I glanced at Ashley. What could it be?

"There is one toy in this store that you must never, ever touch," Candy went on in a hushed voice.

"Which one?" I asked.

"Follow me," Candy said. "I'll show you."

2

TOY OF THE YEAR

Candy led us up an escalator that looked like a toy train.

"I wonder which toy it is," I whispered to Ashley. "And I wonder why we can't touch it."

When we reached the second floor, Candy led us to the back. I saw a neon sign flashing: TOY OF THE YEAR!

"It's got to be Margie," Samantha said.

But two men were blocking the display. They were wearing bright red jackets and black pants and had high black helmets on their heads. They looked just like toy soldiers!

They were each wearing a nametag. I read them aloud: "'Percy' and 'Perry.'"

"What's the password?" Perry asked.

"Gumdrop," Candy replied.

The soldiers each took a step to the side. Between them was a glass case on a platform.

Inside the case was a feathery green bird with bulging eyeballs. It had a chubby belly and skinny legs and arms. Its round feathery head tilted from side to side as it began to sing: "*Let it snow! Let it snow! Let it snoooow!*"

When the doll hit a high note, its feathers stuck straight out. It looked like a bright green powder puff!

"That's Sing-along Sammy!" Ashley cried.

"He's so cool!" I took a step toward the glass case.

An ear-splitting alarm filled the store.

Then a voice boomed over a loudspeaker: "STAND BACK! STAND BACK!"

"Okay, okay!" I quickly jumped back.

"What's the big deal?" Patty said. "You would think he was the last Sammy on earth."

Candy gave us a serious look. "Well, actually, he *is* the last Sing-along Sammy on earth."

Melvin clicked on his tape recorder and began to speak. "Last Sing-along Sammy on earth. One—"

"Oh, no, you don't!" Patty interrupted. "This is *my* party—so *I'm* going to get the last Sammy on earth!"

"In your dreams," Melvin snapped. "My dad will buy me anything I want. And I want Sammy!"

"Forget it, kids," Candy said. "Sammy is not for sale. We want to keep him here, so people from all over the country will come to see him." She smiled at us. "Now remember, after we leave Sammy, you are not to go near him again. Okay?"

Everyone nodded.

The soldiers snapped together in front of Sammy. They meant business!

"Now let's check out all the toys and games you *can* play with," Candy said. "First stop: Rocco's Magic Hut!"

"Yay!" Patty clapped.

Her friends from the Sunshine Scouts jumped and cheered as we headed toward the Magic Hut.

Ashley and I spotted Melvin trying to sneak one last peek at Sing-along Sammy.

"That's one toy Melvin won't be getting this Christmas," Ashley said.

"Who cares about Sammy anyway?" Samantha said. "I still think Margie is cooler."

Another display caught my eye on the way to Rocco's Magic Hut. It was a bedroom set decorated with a white frilly bed, a pink swivel chair, and a fuzzy orange rug.

Ashley, Samantha, and I hung back to check it out.

"That looks just like Margie's Marvelous Bedroom!" Samantha cried. "It's so awesome!"

"Did someone say my name?" a perky voice called. A woman with long blond hair stepped out of her walk-in closet. She was wearing a shiny red dress with white fur trim. "Hi, kids! I'm Margie. Did you happen to see my feathery slippers?"

Ashley and I giggled and shook our heads. The woman looked just like the Margie doll!

"I can't decide what to wear to the party," Margie said. "Will you help me pick out a fabulous outfit later?"

I knew she wasn't really Margie. But it was fun to play along. "Sure!" I said.

"Sounds like fun," Ashley agreed.

But Samantha seemed concerned. "Margie, what happened?" she asked. "How come you're not Toy of the Year anymore?"

Margie's smile disappeared. "I *was* Toy of the Year," she snapped. "Until the day that green feather duster came along."

"You mean Sammy?" Ashley asked.

"Sammy's cool," I said. "And he's a pretty good singer, too."

Margie's face turned as red as her glossy nail polish. "But I have over five hundred outfits!" she cried. "And I don't run on batteries!"

Uh-oh. I had the feeling Margie was a little jealous of all the attention Sammy was getting. Or maybe a *lot* jealous.

"We'd better go and catch up with the others now," Ashley said. "See you later, Margie."

"Toodles!" Margie put a smile back on her face. She gave us a little wave good-bye.

We found Candy and the other kids in front of a blue velvet tent. A sign hanging over the door read, "Magician at Work."

"Kids," Candy announced excitedly. Her

earrings jingled as she pointed to the tent. "You are about to enter the wonderful, exciting world of Rocco's Magic Hut."

Everyone entered the tent. My eyes widened as I looked around. The room had shelves packed with magic wands, top hats, and tons of magic toys and games!

"Where's Rocco?" Alexis asked.

Another door at the back of the tent flapped open. A man wearing a black cape, top hat, and white gloves stepped out. "Greetings," he said. "I am Rocco the Great. And I am about to amaze you with my magic tricks!"

Rocco picked up a Big Tough Toy Truck. He placed it on a small round table covered with a starry tablecloth.

Then Rocco waved his cape over the truck. When he whipped it back, the truck had vanished!

Samantha gasped. "How did he do that?"

Next Rocco opened a tall black box

leaning next to a side of the tent. It was empty. He closed the door to the box and knocked on it three times. Then he yanked it open again.

"Ta-daaa!" Rocco declared.

Everyone gasped. Inside the box was the Big Tough Toy Truck!

"I know that trick," Ashley cried. "I know how he did it!"

Rocco raised an eyebrow. "Oh, really?" he said. "Do you know how I do this?" He whipped his cape over a long table. In a flash, platters of cookies, brownies, and cupcakes appeared!

"Whoa," Ashley said. "Good one."

Tim grabbed a cookie. "Rocco rules. And so do his cookies!"

"Hey, Rocco!" Patty said excitedly. "Why don't you wave your wand and make more Sing-along Sammys appear? Then everybody could have one."

"Yeah!" the Sunshine Scouts chimed in.

"Why is Sing-along Sammy so valuable anyway?" Tim asked. "He's just a goofy toy."

"Are you kidding?" Rocco asked. "I know a guy who collects rare and valuable toys. He'd pay thousands of dollars for the last Sammy on earth."

"Even *my* dad wouldn't pay that much for Sammy," Melvin said sadly. "No matter how much I begged."

Everyone grabbed some more cookies. Then we all went downstairs for the first game of the night.

"Now that your tummies are full," Candy announced, jingling her earrings, "get ready for Santa Belly Limbo!"

I heard another jingle. But it didn't come from Candy's direction. I spun around and saw a little guy peek out from behind the Christmas tree. He was wearing a green cap and a red velvet suit studded with tiny silver bells.

"Hey, look!" I cried. "It's an elf!"

The elf looked surprised as everyone stared at him.

"Are you Tiny?" Candy asked the elf. "From the Holly Jolly Agency?"

"The one and only," Tiny replied. The bells on his cap jingled as he nodded his head.

"Well, thank goodness you're here," Candy said. "You were supposed to hand out candy canes to the kids ages ago."

"Candy canes?" Tiny repeated. He snapped his fingers. "Ah, yes—candy canes!"

He reached into his pocket and pulled out a handful of candy canes. Then he handed one to each of us.

"Only one?" Tim complained.

"There'll be plenty of other goodies for you later," Candy said. "In fact, Tiny was just about to bring out the gingerbread house, weren't you, Tiny?"

"Gingerbread house?" Tiny asked. "Why, there's nothing in the world I'd rather do!" Tiny kicked up his jingly shoes. He whistled a Christmas song as he skipped away.

"He sure is cheerful," Ashley said.

"Of course he's cheerful," Tim said. "Have you ever met a *crabby* elf?" He ate his candy cane in two bites.

I giggled. If there were ever a candy-eating contest, Tim would definitely win!

"Now it's Santa Belly Limbo time!" Candy announced. "Ho, ho, ho! How low can you go?"

Everyone chattered and giggled as they strapped puffy pillows to their bellies. Everyone except Melvin.

"I'm not playing this dumb game," he snapped. "I'd rather work on my Christmas list."

"I wish Rocco would make *Melvin* disappear," Patty grumbled as her cousin stomped away. "He's ruining my whole party. Everyone has to play!"

"Don't worry, Patty," I said. "Ashley and I will find Melvin and bring him back."

"Sure," Ashley said. "You guys start the game without us."

Ashley and I searched the store for Melvin. We checked out the Outer Space Place, the Arts and Crafts Shaft, and the Hula Hoop Hoopla. But we couldn't find him anywhere.

"Where did he go?" Ashley asked.

"Let's ask the toy soldiers guarding Sammy," I suggested. "Maybe they saw Melvin."

Ashley shook her head. "You heard what Candy said, Mary-Kate. We're not allowed to go near Sing-along Sammy."

"We won't go near Sammy," I said. "We'll just peek our heads in and ask."

Ashley and I headed to the Toy of the Year display. But when we got there, something was terribly wrong.

The toy soldiers were gone.

And so was Sammy!

A Christmas Mystery

I stared wide-eyed at the empty glass case. "He's gone!" I cried. "Sammy is gone!"

"Did someone say Sammy's gone?" a panicky voice asked.

I whirled around. Percy and Perry were standing behind us. Perry had a mini-marshmallow stuck to his upper lip.

"He *is* gone!" Percy cried.

"Oh, great," Perry whined. "I told you that hot cocoa break was a bad idea."

"It was *your* idea!" Percy argued.

"Quit it, you guys," Ashley demanded. "We have to find out what happened to Sing-along Sammy."

"Why didn't the alarm go off?" I asked.

"We have no idea!" Perry wailed.

Ashley and I searched around Sammy's platform and found our answer.

"Aha!" I said, picking up two pieces of wire. "Someone cut the wire to the alarm."

"Then it looks like somebody *stole* Sammy," Ashley said. "We have to stop the thief before he or she leaves the building!"

"Don't worry," Percy said. "No one can get in or out until the morning. All the doors were locked to keep out party crashers."

"Then whoever stole Sammy is still in the store," I said. "But who's the thief?"

"Look!" Ashley exclaimed. She pointed to a bright pink smear on the glass. "I bet the thief left that smudge behind."

"But what's the pink stuff?" I asked.

Ashley leaned forward and took a whiff.

"It smells sweet," she said. "Kind of like strawberries."

I reached out and touched the smudge. "And it feels sticky," I pointed out.

"Sweet? Sticky? We're wasting our time!" Percy cried. "We should be looking for Sammy!"

"Sammy was our responsibility," Perry said. "When the owner of the store finds out we lost him, we'll lose our jobs!"

"Ashley and I are detectives," I told them. "We'll do our best to find Sing-along Sammy."

"But for now, why don't you two stand in front of Sammy's case?" Ashley suggested. "So no one can see that he's missing."

Perry and Percy marched to the display. They clicked their heels and moved in front of the glass case.

"There's another reason we have to find Sammy quick," Ashley whispered to me. "If the others find out Sammy is missing, then Patty's sleepover will be totally ruined."

"Maybe we should just tell Tim and Samantha," I suggested. "They've helped us with our cases before. Maybe they can help us find Sammy!"

"Good idea," Ashley said. "But first, let's figure out what we already know."

She reached into the pocket of her jeans for her pen and detective pad.

"We know that Sammy is very expensive," Ashley said. "So lots of people would love to have him."

"Except Margie," I pointed out. "She would rather get *rid* of Sammy. So she could be Toy of the Year again."

Ashley nodded and wrote Margie's name on her pad. Then her eyes lit up. "Hey—what about Rocco?" she asked. "He knows a guy who collects rare and valuable toys. If Rocco sold the last Sammy to him, he'd be rich!"

"And there's somebody else," I said. "Patty's cousin, Melvin. He really wanted Sing-along Sammy, too."

"True," Ashley agreed. "But almost *all* the kids here wanted Sing-along Sammy. When it comes to Melvin, we need more evidence."

I smiled to myself. Ashley and I look pretty much alike. But when it comes to solving mysteries, we're as different as night and day. Ashley likes to think about all possibilities before making a move. I like to make a move, then consider the possibilities!

"But we do know the thief had pink stuff on his or her hands," I said. "So let's keep our eyes open for smudgy fingers."

Tim and Samantha ran over. They were wearing white beards, and puffy pillows were strapped to their bellies.

"Patty sent us to get you," Tim said.

"Yeah. What's taking you so long?" Samantha asked us.

"We have a mystery!" I declared.

Tim and Samantha listened while I told

them about Sing-along Sammy. Then Ashley clued them in on our suspects.

"Wow!" Tim exclaimed. "This party is going to be more exciting than I thought."

The four of us went back down to the party. This time, instead of using the train escalator, we slid down a red-and-white-striped candy-cane pole!

"There you are," Patty said when we reached the bottom. "You both missed the game, and I won!"

"You won?" Ashley asked. "Congratulations, Patty!"

"Thanks," Patty said. "Now, where's my cousin Melvin?"

"M-Melvin?" I glanced at Ashley. We were so busy discussing the case that we forgot to bring Melvin back to the party!

Ashley shrugged. "We…uh—"

"Look out below!" Melvin yelled from the top of the candy-cane pole. He jumped on it and slid down fast.

Ashley and I jumped back as Melvin landed with a thud!

"Where were you?" Patty demanded.

"Working on my Christmas list," Melvin said. "And I bet I'll get everything on it, too!"

But when Melvin stepped away from the candy-cane pole, I saw something that made my stomach flip. Melvin had left smudgy streaks up and down the pole.

Pink smudgy streaks!

NUMBER ONE SUSPECT

I nudged Ashley and pointed to the pole. "Is that enough evidence for you?" I whispered.

"It's a clue, all right," Ashley whispered back. "And Melvin is our number one suspect."

While the others pulled off their Santa bellies and beards, Ashley and I studied Melvin. He was busy adding more toys and games to his Christmas list.

"Hey, everybody, look!" Candy announced. "Tiny has our gingerbread house!"

"Ta-daaa!" Tiny sang as he rolled the gingerbread house over on a cart.

The yummy-looking house was incredible. It was covered with all kinds of frosting— vanilla, chocolate, strawberry, and lemon!

"Can we eat it now?" Tim asked.

"Not yet," Candy said. "I think Margie has an announcement to make."

Margie's high heels clicked on the floor as she hurried over to the group. "Hey, kids!" she said. "Who wants to help me pick out a glamorous outfit to wear to the party?"

"Me! Me! Me!" Patty, Samantha, and the Sunshine Scouts shouted.

"Then let's all go to my Marvelous Bedroom and start stylin'!" Margie declared.

"No way," Melvin said. "I didn't come here to play with *dolls*!"

"There he goes again," Patty complained as Melvin stomped away.

"Let's follow him," I whispered to Ashley. We turned to chase Melvin.

"Where are you two going?" Patty demanded.

My sister and I froze. "We…uh—"

"You already missed the Santa Belly Limbo," Patty complained. "If you skip another game, I'll never speak to you again!"

"How are we supposed to follow Melvin if we're partying with Patty?" Ashley whispered to me.

Tim heard her. "Don't worry," he said. "I'll spy on Melvin and see what he's up to."

"Thanks, Tim," Ashley whispered.

"No problem," Tim said. Then he sneaked away from the group.

"Hey, I have an idea," I told Ashley. "Let's search Margie's Marvelous Bedroom. If Margie stole Sammy there's a good chance she hid him in there."

"Right," Ashley said. "Let's go."

While the other girls were looking for a cool outfit for Margie, Ashley and I tried to find Sammy.

"Anything?" Ashley whispered as we hunted through Margie's Wondrous Wardrobe.

"Tons of shoes, handbags, pants, and skirts." I sighed. "But no Sammy."

I looked around the room. Next to Margie's bed was an orange night table with a big drawer.

"We haven't searched that night table yet," I said. "Let's go for it." I reached out to open the drawer.

"Don't open that!" Margie shouted.

"Why?" I asked.

"Why?" Margie repeated. She flashed a big smile. "Because I have everything I need for the party!"

Margie showed off her outfit: a short silver dress, matching shoes with skinny heels, and a shiny red belt.

"Did you see that?" Ashley murmured. "Margie does not want us near the night table."

"Which makes me think she's hiding

something in there," I answered.

Margie crossed to the middle of the room. "My new party outfit *rocks*!" she declared. "And because you all were such a big help—I'm going to share my latest beauty secret with you!"

She grabbed a swivel chair that faced a full-length mirror. Then she swung it all the way around. "Ta-daaa!" Margie sang.

Patty was sitting in the chair. She had a creamy beauty mask on her face.

I grabbed Ashley's arm. "Check out that cream. It's *pink*!"

"It's the same color as the smudgy fingerprint," Ashley added.

Samantha noticed the color of the cream, too. She inched her way over to us. "You guys," she said slowly. "Do you think *Patty* could be a suspect?"

5

SNIFFING OUT CLUES

Ashley and I stared at the creamy pink mask on Patty's face.

Could Patty really be a suspect? I wondered. She *did* say she wanted the last Sammy on earth. But then I thought of something else.

"No," I told Samantha. "Patty can't be a suspect. She was playing Santa Belly Limbo when Sammy was stolen. And the beauty mask belongs to Margie."

"Right," Ashley agreed. "Which means

that *Margie* is our suspect, not Patty."

"Come on, girls!" Margie cried. "Let's get fabulous!"

The Sunshine Scouts lined up as Margie slathered pink cream on their noses, chins, and cheeks.

"Time for another sniff test," I whispered. "If the cream smells sweet, then we've got evidence against Margie."

Ashley, Samantha, and I joined the line.

"Hi!" Margie said. She dipped her finger in the creamy jar. "Try my new Pretty in Pink Dream Cream!"

I took a step back. I didn't want a ton of cream on my face. I just wanted answers to my questions.

"Did *you* use the cream today, Margie?" I asked her.

Margie reached up and stroked her cheek. "Can't you tell?" she asked. "I used it about an hour ago and my face feels silky and soft."

An hour ago? My heart did a triple flip. That was about the time Sammy disappeared!

"Would you girls like to try my face mask?" Margie asked.

"Uh…not until we smell it first," Ashley blurted out.

Margie wrinkled her nose. "You want to *smell* my beauty mask?"

"Yeah," I said, trying to think quick. "You see…we can't stand the smell of…uh—"

"Onions!" Samantha cut in. "If it smells like onions, we'll totally barf."

Margie gasped. "Oh, um, help yourselves." She screwed the lid onto the jar and tossed it to me. Then she turned to the other girls. "Come on, girlfriends. Let's party on!"

Margie and the others filed out of the bedroom.

"I'd better go, too," Samantha said. "If the three of us are missing, Patty will really get suspicious."

Samantha ran to catch up. Ashley and I got right down to business.

"You sniff the Dream Cream," Ashley said. "I'm going to look inside that night table for Sammy."

I unscrewed the lid and took a whiff. It didn't smell like strawberries at all. It smelled like *peppermint*!

"Hey, Ashley," I called. "This can't be the same stuff we found on the glass case."

"Mary-Kate!" Ashley called. "Get over here fast!"

I rushed over to my sister. She was staring down at the floor next to Margie's bed. I followed her gaze.

A clump of green feathers was sticking out from under the frilly bed.

I gasped. "It's Sing-along Sammy!"

Making the Call

6

"**M**argie stole Sing-along Sammy," I told Ashley. "Case closed." I reached down to grab Sammy's fuzzy green feathers. "Well, that was easiest case we ever—"

"Hey! Why are you snooping around in my bedroom?" Margie shouted.

Oops! We were caught. Ashley and I turned around slowly.

"We…uh—" Ashley began.

Then I stepped in. "We know you stole Sing-along Sammy," I told Margie.

"But Mary-Kate…" Ashley said.

"*And* we have proof!" I added.

"Me?" Margie asked. She rolled her eyes. "The last thing I'd want is Sing-along Sammy!"

"Oh, yeah? Then how do you explain *this*?" I reached under Margie's bed for Sammy. But I couldn't find him. I flipped up the bedspread to get a look. There was nothing under there. Where did the parrot go?

"Uh, Mary-Kate?" Ashley asked.

"Yes?" I turned to her.

Ashley held up a fuzzy green shoe. "I don't think this is Sammy," she said.

My face suddenly grew hot. "Oh. Okay."

"My feathery slipper!" Margie cried happily. "Thanks a million for finding it."

"No problem," I said. I tried to hide my disappointment. But it wasn't easy.

"Why would you think *I'd* want to steal Sing-along Sammy?" Margie asked.

"Because you acted kind of jealous,"

Ashley explained. "We thought you were angry because he's Toy of the Year."

"And maybe you thought Sammy might make you lose your job," I added. "Honolulu Hal and Cricket got fired because they're not popular anymore."

Ashley nodded. "And right now Sammy is stealing the show. He's the most famous toy ever!"

Margie threw back her blond head and began to laugh.

"What's so funny?" I asked.

"I'm through with being a living doll," Margie declared. "Starting tomorrow, I'll be a Flaky Girl!"

"A Flaky Girl?" I repeated.

Margie explained that her real name was Vicki. And that she'd just gotten a part as a dancing snowflake in the new Sally Swan Spectacular Show.

Vicki walked to the night table and opened the drawer. "Here's my letter of resignation."

Ashley took the letter and read it out loud. "'Dear Tower of Toys, I quit!' Signed, 'Vicki Martin.'"

It was short and to the point. But most of all, it showed that Vicki had no reason to steal Sammy.

"Thanks for sharing your secret with us, Vicki," I said. "And good luck being a Flaky Girl."

"Well, I'm not a Flaky Girl until tomorrow," Vicki said. "I'll see you at the party— as soon as I find my satin handbag!"

We left Margie's Marvelous Bedroom and headed to the train escalator. "No wonder Vicki didn't want us near the night table," I said. "That's where she kept her secret letter."

Ashley pulled out her detective pad. She crossed Margie's name off her suspect list. "One down, two to go," she said. "Melvin and Rocco the Great."

I stopped in front of Rocco's blue velvet tent. "Let's check out the Magic Hut for clues before we go back to the party."

Ashley and I slipped inside. Rocco wasn't in the Magic Hut, so the coast was clear.

The first thing I noticed was the cookies on the table. "They're all white and green with red sprinkles." I sighed. "No pink frosting."

Next I saw Rocco's tall black hat sitting on a small round table. "Where's Rocco?" I wondered out loud.

"Shh!" Ashley whispered. "I think I hear someone."

I listened closely. Rocco's voice was coming from behind the back door. It sounded like he was talking on the phone.

"Hello, Wally?" Rocco was saying. "Remember that toy you wanted so badly? Well, guess what? I got it for you!"

"Did you hear that, Ashley?" I whispered. "Wally must be that toy collector guy! I bet Rocco is talking about Sing-along Sammy!"

Ashley put her finger to her lips to signal

that we had to be quiet. I nodded.

"I can't talk long, Wally," Rocco said. "I've got to get back to the party."

I heard Rocco say good-bye. I wanted to look for more clues. But I didn't want Rocco to see us. "Ashley, quick!" I whispered. "Under the table!"

Ashley and I ducked under the cookie table. The tablecloth was long enough to hide us. I lifted the edge of the cloth and peeked out.

Rocco was now in the tent. He placed his cell phone on the small round table next to his tall black hat.

Ashley and I waited until Rocco left the Magic Hut. Then we scurried out from under the table.

"If Rocco took Sammy, then he probably hid him somewhere," Ashley said. She pointed to the tall black hat on the table. "Like maybe inside his hat!"

Ashley ran to the table. She rolled up her

sleeve and stuck her hand way down the hat. "Hey!" she called. "I feel something. It's soft. And fuzzy!"

"Sammy is soft and fuzzy!" I cried.

Ashley yelped as she pulled out a white furry rabbit. "Whoa!" she said. She put the rabbit back where she found it.

I glanced at Rocco's cell phone. It was the same kind of phone that Great-Grandma Olive used.

"This phone stores all the last numbers that you call," I told Ashley. "Maybe we can trace Wally."

"Go for it," Ashley said.

I entered a few codes on the keypad. A number flashed on the tiny screen.

"This must be it," I said. Then I pressed the Call button.

Ashley listened over my shoulder.

"Hello?" a voice squeaked. It didn't sound like a toy collector. It sounded like a little boy!

"Hi," I said. "Is Wally home?"

"I'm Wally!" the boy said. "Who's this?"

Ashley and I looked at each other.

"Maybe Wally is Rocco's son," Ashley whispered. "And Rocco stole Sing-along Sammy for *him*!"

That was a good point. So I decided to ask some questions.

"My name is Mary-Kate," I told the boy. "By any chance…is your dad a magician?"

"The best," Wally answered. "He's Rocco the Great."

Ashley was right! I thought. "And did you want a Sing-along Sammy for Christmas?" I held my breath and waited for an answer.

"No way!" Wally said. "My dad got me a Laugh-It-Up-Larry. He laughs so hard that his eyes pop out. Is that neat, or what?"

"Totally neat." I sighed.

"Hey—I just remembered something," Wally said. "I'm not allowed to talk to strangers. Bye!" He hung up.

I turned to Ashley. "Rocco was never talking to his collector friend," I said. "And he wasn't talking about Sing-along Sammy. Now what do we do?"

"Well, Rocco still *has* a collector friend," Ashley said. "Which means he still might have stolen Sammy for him."

"Right!" I said. The search for Sammy went on. I looked behind the door. There were more capes and hats hanging on hooks, but no Sammy. Ashley peeked inside a tall wicker basket. There was a bunch of rubber chickens but no Sammy.

"I'm going to look inside the big black box," Ashley said. "You know, where Rocco made the Big Tough Toy Truck appear." She opened the door and crept inside the box.

Meanwhile, I checked out shelves. All I found were wands, Magic 8-balls, and trick card decks. "Sammy, where are you?" I groaned. I stepped back and bumped into something.

SLAM!

"Hey!" Ashley cried.

I whirled around and gulped. I had accidentally shut the door of the big black box—with Ashley still inside!

"Sorry, Ashley." I grabbed the handle and pulled open the door. But the box was empty—and Ashley was *gone*!

"Oh, no," I cried. "I made my sister disappear!"

7

A DISAPPEARING ACT

My heart pounded as I groped inside the empty box. Was the box really magic? And if it was—how would I get my sister back?

"Ashley, where are you?" I cried.

No answer. There was just one thing left to do.

"Help!" I shouted. "Helllp!"

The velvet curtain swung open and Rocco stepped inside. "What's the matter?" he asked.

"Please, Rocco," I said, pointing to the

box. "You have to bring my sister back!"

"Oh, my," Rocco said. "Was your sister inside that magic box? All right, then."

Rocco shut the door of the black box. He knocked three times on the door. Next Rocco waved his wand over the box. He pulled the door open—and I smiled.

Ashley was sitting inside.

"Ashley!" I cried. "You're okay!"

Ashley grinned and jumped out of the box. "I told you I knew how that trick works," she said. "I was right. There's a secret door in there!"

Rocco held up a white-gloved finger. "But that trick will be our little secret, right?"

"You bet," Ashley said.

But I couldn't stop staring at Rocco's hands. There was something about them that didn't add up. Then I figured out what it was! "Ashley, we should get back to the party," I said. "Thanks, Rocco. Bye!"

Ashley seemed confused as I whisked

her out of the Magic Hut. "Mary-Kate?" she asked. "Aren't we going to question Rocco about Sing-along Sammy?"

I shook my head. "Rocco couldn't have left that pink fingerprint on the glass case," I said. "Rocco wears *gloves!*"

"Unless," Ashley said, "Rocco took off the gloves before he stole Sammy."

"Remember what Great-Grandma Olive once told us?" I asked. "Criminals usually put gloves *on* before committing a crime."

"Right. So they don't leave fingerprints," Ashley added. "It wouldn't make sense for Rocco to take off his gloves to steal something. Good catch, Mary-Kate!"

"Now we have only one suspect left," I said.

"Melvin," Ashley said. "Let's hope that Tim is doing a good job watching him."

Ashley and I hurried back to the party. Everyone was dancing to a rocking version of "Jingle Bells." I spotted Samantha and

Tim dancing on top of a giant toy drum.

"Tim, what are you doing up there?" I called to him. "I thought you were supposed to follow Melvin."

Tim and Samantha jumped down from the drum.

"I did," Tim said. "And you're not going to believe what happened."

"What?" Ashley and I asked at the same time.

"I saw Melvin steal a bunch of toys!" Tim whispered.

"Wow!" Ashley exclaimed. "Maybe Sing-along Sammy is with the rest of the stolen toys!"

"Where did Melvin hide them?" I asked.

Tim shrugged. "I don't know," he said. "After he stole three whirly-copters, I lost him."

"You lost him?" Ashley cried.

Tim pulled a handful of caramels from his pocket. "I passed by the Snack Shack and had to stop," he said. "They had tons of my favorite treats."

Ashley and I groaned.

"Oh, well," Samantha said. "At least you have some new information about Melvin. You know he's a thief."

I felt Patty tap my shoulder.

"You just missed Jingle Bell Charades, Pass the Snowball, and the Ho-Ho-Hokey Pokey!" Patty said. "You're just as bad as Melvin—he keeps disappearing, too!"

This time I couldn't blame Patty for being angry. It seemed as though we were awful party guests.

"We're sorry, Patty," I said.

"We promise we'll play the next game," Ashley said.

The music ended and Candy clapped her hands for attention. "I hope you like reindeer games, because it's time to play Pin the Nose on Rudolph!" she announced.

Tiny lugged over an easel and a big

poster of Rudolph the Red-nosed Reindeer. But instead of a red nose, Rudolph had a square piece of Velcro on his face.

Candy held up a small red ball and a blindfold. "Whoever sticks the nose closest to the right spot wins," she explained. "Who wants to go first?"

"Pick Mary-Kate or Ashley!" Patty insisted.

"I'll go first," I said.

Candy tossed me the sticky red ball. She tied a blindfold across my eyes and turned me around and around.

"Okay, Mary-Kate!" Candy cheered. "Pin the nose on Rudolph!"

I couldn't see a thing. But I could hear everyone giggling and whispering as I tried to find Rudolph.

I waved my hands in front of me and stumbled around. Someone giggled when I grabbed her shoulder. I walked in the other direction and felt something prickly.

"It's the Christmas tree!" someone cried.

"Whoops!" I giggled.

I walked in another direction and caught a whiff of something sweet. *It smells like strawberries*, I realized. And Ashley had said the pink fingerprint smelled like strawberries!

This is definitely a clue, I thought. The farther I walked, the stronger the scent got. If I could just figure out what the strawberry stuff was, maybe I'd find out who stole Sammy!

I reached in front of me and took a few more steps.

"Mary-Kate!" Ashley yelled. *"Stop!"*

8

HIDING THE EVIDENCE

"**H**uh?" I gasped.

I froze in place and pulled down the blindfold. I was two inches away from the cart with the gingerbread house on it!

"You almost knocked down our gingerbread house," Patty complained. "And you lose because you cheated. You pulled down your blindfold!"

I didn't care much about losing. All I could think about was that sweet strawberry smell. Did the gingerbread house have anything to do with the pink fingerprint?

"We'd better move this out of the way for now," Candy said. She rolled the ginger-bread house to the side.

As the game went on, I whispered my discovery to Ashley. She wanted to sniff the gingerbread house, too, but no way could we leave the game now.

"I won! I won!" Tim shouted after he pinned the nose right in the center of Rudolph's face.

Candy handed Tim his prize: a jar of glow-in-the-dark rubber worms.

"What are we going to do next, Candy?" Patty asked.

"'Tis the season to say cheese," Candy said. She held up a camera. "Are you all ready for the group picture?"

Everyone nodded.

"Great!" Candy said. "Then why don't you all gather around the big snowman and look jolly?"

I glanced over at the fake snowman. It was still surrounded by sleeping bags and backpacks.

"We can't," Kendra said. "That's where we piled all our stuff."

Candy put two fingers in her mouth and gave a shrill whistle. I heard a jingle as Tiny rushed over.

"Tiny," Candy said. "Please move the sleeping bags and backpacks so we can take a picture by the snowman."

"Okey-dokey!" Tiny said. He marched over to the sleeping-bag rolls and tossed them aside one by one. But just as he reached for a big, fat orange one, Melvin screamed.

"Don't touch my sleeping bag!" Melvin yelled. He grabbed his orange sleeping bag and dragged it to the side. "The only one who's going to touch my sleeping bag is *me*! Got that?"

Tiny seemed to force a smile. "Okey-dokey!" he repeated.

Everyone stared at Melvin. What was his problem?

"You would think Melvin would want someone to help him with his sleeping bag," I whispered to Ashley. "It's so big and bulky!"

"It *is* bulky," Ashley whispered back. "As if something is rolled up inside...but *what*?"

"Maybe it's something that Melvin wants to *hide*," I whispered to Ashley. "I bet he stashed Sammy and the other stolen toys inside his sleeping bag. We have to unroll it and find out."

Ashley nodded. "We'll do it right after Candy takes the picture."

After the sleeping bags were moved, Tiny skipped away.

Candy held up the camera and smiled. "Ready?" she asked.

"Yes," Patty said. "But I don't think we should pose in front of the snowman."

"Then where?" Candy asked.

Patty stuck her chin in the air. "I want to have our picture taken with *Sing-along Sammy,*" she announced.

"Cool!" Maria said. "That's a great idea, Patty."

The other Sunshine Scouts seemed to agree.

Ashley and I stared at each other. Patty couldn't have her picture taken with Sammy—because there *was* no Sammy!

9

CAUGHT ON TAPE

"**P**atty, we're not supposed to go near Sammy tonight," Candy said.

Patty stomped her right foot on the ground. "This is my party and I want to have our picture taken with the last Sammy on earth!"

"Well." Candy sighed. "I guess it wouldn't hurt to take just one picture."

I quickly looked at Samantha for help.

"Patty!" Samantha called out. "If we're going to have our picture taken with Sing-along Sammy, then we all need to look extra special!"

"Extra special?" Patty repeated.

Samantha waved a hand toward the Tower of Toys Costume Corner. "We need costumes!" she declared.

"Samantha's right," Tim agreed. "Maybe we can even get our picture with Sammy in a newspaper—or a magazine!"

"We'll be famous!" Patty shrieked.

She and the Sunshine Scouts began jumping up and down.

"All right, then," Candy announced. Her earrings jingled as she nodded. "Everybody to the Costume Corner!"

"No way!" Melvin growled. "I don't play dress-up."

Uh-oh. We had to keep Melvin busy while we searched his sleeping bag.

"Um—but there's a perfect costume for you, Melvin!" I blurted out. "You can be Captain Superdude!"

"Captain Superdude?" Melvin said. "He's my favorite TV hero. He totally rules!"

"Then, go for it!" I smiled.

Ashley and I hung back while the others raced to the Costume Corner.

"That should keep them busy for a while," I said. "Now let's search Melvin's sleeping bag!"

We hurried over to the bag. Ashley unrolled it and we looked inside.

Just as we had suspected, there was a stash of small toys and games. "These must be the stolen toys that Tim was talking about," I said.

We hunted through the toys, hoping to find Sing-along Sammy.

"The only green thing is that," Ashley said, pointing to a rubber head with bulging eyes and a gaping mouth. "What is it?"

"It's an Alien Gross Gusher," I replied. "I saw it on TV."

"An alien—*what*?" Ashley asked.

I smiled and picked up the gross rubber

head. "I think you have to squeeze it and—"

GUSH!

Ashley shrieked as a glob of slime shot out of the alien's mouth. She ducked just as it splattered on the wall behind her.

"Sorry I asked." Ashley groaned.

I stared at the drippy goo.

The gooey, drippy *pink* goo.

"I'm not," I said. "Look at the color of that slime. We've got more evidence against Melvin. Maybe he touched the Alien Gross Gusher right before he took Sammy!"

"We still need more proof," Ashley said. "Let's check out that goo."

We were just about to do that when Melvin ran over. He was dressed in a blue leotard, yellow cape, and black sunglasses.

"What are you doing with my stuff?" Melvin demanded.

"*Your* stuff?" Ashley asked. She pointed to the toys in his sleeping bag. "These games belong to Tower of Toys!"

"So?" Melvin shrugged.

"So did you steal them?" Ashley demanded.

"*Steal?*" Melvin exclaimed. "No way!"

"Then how did they get inside your sleeping bag?" I asked Melvin.

"Candy told us we could each keep one toy," Melvin explained. "I was just holding on to these toys until I decided which one I really wanted."

That explained the toys in the sleeping bag. But it still didn't explain another toy. A *missing* toy!

"We know that Sing-along Sammy is missing," I said. "Did you hide him, too?"

Melvin gasped. "I didn't know Sammy was missing. And I didn't take him, either!"

I wasn't sure I believed him. "Were you anywhere near Sammy's glass case while the soldiers took a break?" I asked Melvin.

"Um." Melvin gulped. "I...er—"

"Well?" I asked.

"Okay, okay," Melvin said. "I did sneak

over to Sammy's case when the toy soldiers took a break. But no way did I steal him!"

"Then what were you doing?" Ashley asked.

"I knew I couldn't have Sing-along Sammy for keeps," Melvin explained. "So I recorded his voice instead."

Ashley and I stared at the tape recorder Melvin carried in his hand. Was he telling the truth?

"Can we hear it, please?" Ashley asked.

"Sure," Melvin said. He switched on the tape recorder and rewound the tape. He stopped at the part where Sammy began to sing: "*Frosty the snowman, was a jolly happy soul! With a—*"

CLICK! The singing stopped.

"What was that click?" I asked. "And what happened to the rest of the song?"

"I stopped recording when I heard footsteps," Melvin explained. "I thought it might be Candy, so I ran away."

"That's funny," I said to Ashley. "If the soldiers were coming, they would have seen Melvin running away from Sammy. And they would have tried to stop him."

"Unless those footsteps weren't the soldiers returning to their post," Ashley said. "Unless those footsteps were from the *thief*!"

"It wasn't the soldiers," Melvin said. "They were still on their hot cocoa break."

"How do you know it wasn't them?" I asked him.

Melvin shrugged. "Because I heard bells jingling."

"And the soldiers don't have bells on their costume," I added. "Boy, this mystery is getting more interesting by the second."

"Yes," Ashley said. "And I think we're about to solve it, too!"

10

JINGLE BELLS

“**T**he thief has to be Candy,” Ashley declared. “She has on those jingle-bell earrings.”

“Oh, right!” I agreed.

But something was bothering me. Why would Candy want to steal Sammy? She seemed so proud that the last Sammy on earth was here at Tower of Toys.

Tim raced over from the Costume Corner. He was wearing a black pirate’s hat and an eye patch. “Everyone is almost finished dressing," he said. "So you'd better solve this case fast."

"We think we already did!" Ashley cried.

Tim listened as we told him everything about the tape recorder, the bells, even Candy.

"Wow! Good work, Melvin," Tim said. "That tape recorder came in way handy."

"I'll say," Melvin said. "I'm going to ask my dad for five more."

Tim smiled as he pulled a candy cane out of his pocket. He unwrapped it and twirled it in his mouth.

"Another candy cane?" I asked. "I thought you already ate yours, Tim."

"I did," Tim said, still slurping.

"Then how did you get that one?" Ashley asked.

"I found it on the floor when we discovered Sammy was missing," Tim explained. "I put it in my pocket in case of a hunger emergency. Pretty smart, huh?"

Ashley and I looked at each other.

"But didn't we get those candy canes *before* Sammy was missing?" I asked.

Ashley nodded. "That means Candy must have dropped it when she stole Sammy." She frowned. "But wait. Candy didn't have any candy canes. She wanted to give them to us earlier in the night, remember?"

"But she had to wait for Tiny the elf to hand them out." I smiled. "He was the one with all the candy canes. And he was late. Probably because he was stealing Sammy!"

"And he's got bells on his costume, too," Ashley pointed out. "I can't believe I forgot that."

"But how does that explain the pink smudgy fingerprint?" Tim asked.

I suddenly remembered the sweet-smelling gingerbread house.

"Tiny brought out the gingerbread house," I said. "And the house was covered with all kinds of frosting."

"Pink frosting!" Tim added.

"*Strawberry* frosting," I said.

"We have our thief!" Ashley cried. "Now, if we can just find Sing-along Sammy, we'll have this case solved."

The four of us made our way to the Costume Corner. Patty was dressed in a princess-style robe, rhinestone tiara, and a long, feathery scarf.

Samantha was holding Patty's arm. And Patty was struggling to break free.

"I said *let go*!" Patty demanded. "I don't want any more glitter in my hair. And I don't want any more costumes. I just want to have my picture taken with Sammy!"

"But you haven't tried on the red glitter shoes yet," Samantha cried.

"I said *no*!" Patty shouted. "I want to go upstairs to Sammy, and I want to go *now*!"

Ashley and I sighed. It was no use keeping Patty in the dark any longer. It was time to tell her the truth.

"You can't, Patty," I said.

"Why not?" Patty snapped. "This is my sleepover party and if I want—"

"Sing-along Sammy is missing," I cut in.

"Missing?" Patty gasped.

"No way!" Alexis cried.

"Sammy can't be missing!" Kendra insisted.

"What?" Candy cried, running over. "Did someone say Sammy is missing?"

"It's true," Ashley explained. "Someone stole Sing-along Sammy from his glass case."

"Who?" Patty gasped.

JINGLE, JINGLE, JINGLE!

I spun around and saw Tiny darting out from behind the Christmas tree.

"*That's* the thief!" Ashley cried. "Get him!"

FOLLOW THAT ELF!

"Cheese and crackers!" Tiny growled. He picked up a huge gift box and began to run.

"He's probably got Sammy inside that box!" I exclaimed.

Ashley, Tim, Samantha, and I chased Tiny through the store. We wove our way between dollhouses, stuffed animals, sports equipment, and book displays. But Tiny was too fast!

"We have to catch him!" Ashley panted.

We rounded the Freaky Frisbee Zone

and picked up speed. But just as we were about to catch up, Tiny jumped on an electric skateboard!

"Let's see you catch me now!" Tiny cackled over his shoulder. "Ha, ha, haaaa!"

Tiny whizzed past shelves of beach pails and water blasters. The big box was still tucked under his arm.

"How are we going to catch up to him?" I groaned.

Tim pointed to a row of shiny metallic scooters. "Those Saber Scooters are lightning fast," he said.

Ashley, Tim, Samantha, and I each grabbed a scooter and strapped on a helmet. Then we jumped aboard and took off!

"We're right behind you, Teeny!" Tim called.

"That's *Tiny*!" the elf yelled over his shoulder. He didn't see the tall tower of plush toys in front of him.

"Tiny—look out!" Ashley shouted.

"Yaaaaa!" Tiny yelped as he whizzed toward the tower of toys. "I can't stop!"

We stared as Tiny went crashing through the pile of soft jungle animals. The gift box flew through the air and landed a few feet away from us.

"Is he okay?" Ashley asked.

"I don't know," I answered.

Candy and the kids came running over. Right behind them were Rocco and Vicki.

Ashley and I stared at the jumbled pile of toys. If Tiny was behind those stuffed animals, why didn't we hear anything?

Then we did—

"Okay, elf," a gruff voice said. "You've got some explaining to do."

I blinked as the two soldiers marched out from behind the pile. They were holding Tiny by his arms.

"Get your hands off me!" Tiny yelled. His bells jingled like crazy as he tried to break free.

"Is this who you're looking for?" Percy asked.

"We heard all the noise down here," Perry said. "So we thought you needed help."

"Thanks," Ashley said. "We think Tiny here might have taken Sing-along Sammy."

"You can't prove it!" Tiny snapped.

"Oh, really?" I picked up the box that Tiny had been carrying.

Ashley pulled the red ribbon loose and whipped off the top. Then she reached inside and pulled out Sing-along Sammy!

"*Deck the halls with boughs of holly!*" Sammy belted out. "*Fa, la, la, la, laaaaaa!*"

"Phooey!" Tiny spat out. "I went through all this trouble for nothing. I could have been rich. Rich!"

"Come on, Tiny," Percy said. "The next bells you'll be hearing will be on a squad car."

The soldiers marched Tiny out of the store.

Candy turned to us and smiled. "I can't thank you girls enough," she said. "You saved the last Sing-along Sammy. And that is definitely something to sing about."

"*Fa, la, la, la, laaaaa!*" Sammy crooned.

"Case closed!" Ashley declared. She looked at the big clock on the wall. "But Patty's sleepover has just begun. It's only midnight."

"Yay!" the Sunshine Scouts cheered.

"Hey," Samantha said, looking around. "Where is Patty, anyway?"

Ashley and I heard a loud snore. We turned and saw Patty leaning against a gift box—fast asleep!

"Oh, well," I whispered. "I guess even princesses need their sleep."

"Yeah." Ashley yawned. "And so do detectives!"

"Everything worked out great," Ashley remembered as she twirled a green ribbon between her fingers. "Patty's sleepover *was* totally awesome."

"So was the case," I said. "But after all that, I don't need to see another Sing-along Sammy for a long time!"

"Me, neither," Ashley agreed.

Our basset hound, Clue, scampered over to us. She began barking and sniffing at a big, tall box.

"Oh!" I said. "We forgot to open that one."

Ashley and I both ripped off the silver-and-green wrapping paper. I smiled when I saw the name on the box.

"Hey," I said. "It's from Tower of Toys."

"Maybe it's two of those scooters!" Ashley said excitedly.

"Or some Alien Gross Gushers," I joked.

We pulled the lid off and groaned. Inside was a green feathery doll. Its head tilted from side to side as it began to sing—

"*Oh, the weather outside is frightful! Let it snow, let it snow, let it snooooow!*"

Clue put her paws over her head and whimpered.

"It's…" Ashley started to say. "It's…"

I opened a note from Candy and read it out loud:

"'Dear Mary-Kate and Ashley. Guess what? We found two hundred Sing-along Sammys in the basement. So there are *plenty* of them to go around!

"'Enjoy…and Merry Christmas!'"

Hi from both of us,

Ashley and I couldn't believe it. We were actually walking down a red carpet, on our way to a fabulous Hollywood awards show! We were about to meet all our favorite television stars—including the dreamy Justin Dare!

We had no idea what we were in for—or that the party would be *nothing* like we thought.

Want to find out what happened? Check out the next page for a sneak peek at *The New Adventures of Mary-Kate & Ashley: The Case of the Hollywood Who-Done-It*.

See you next time!

Mary-Kate Olsen   *Ashley Olsen*

The New Adventures of MARY-KATE & ASHLEY

A sneak peek at our next mystery…

The Case Of The
HOLLYWOOD WHO-DONE-IT

"This is too good to be true," I whispered to Ashley. We were actually at the Holly awards talking to our favorite actor, Justin Dare and his stuntman, Roger Lorre!

"So what's it like to be in the running for best actor?" I asked Justin.

Roger sniffed. "Oh, please," he said. "I was in the movie more than Justin was. *I* should be the one running for best actor!"

"No way," Justin replied. "I'm the real star. You're just a stuntman."

"Take that back!" Roger shouted. He gave Justin a shove.

Justin stumbled into the table holding

the Best Actor and Actress Hollys. *Bam! Bam!* The Hollys fell to the ground.

"Look what you made me do!" Justin climbed to his feet and launched himself at Roger.

Roger crashed into the huge ice sculpture that was shaped like a Holly statue. The ice sculpture wobbled. It tilted left. It tilted right. Then it fell over.

Ka-bam! The sculpture slammed into the wall. It knocked the light switches off on its way to the floor.

The room went black. Ashley and I grabbed each other's arms.

A few minutes later, the lights switched back on. Mr. Martinez, the director of the show, came running across the room. "Nobody move!" he shouted. "The Best Actor and Actress Hollys have been stolen!"

WIN A MARY-KATE AND ASHLEY
Best Friends Prize Pack!

....

WIN <u>TWO</u> OF EACH OF THE FABULOUS PRIZES LISTED BELOW:
One set for you, one set for your best buddy! It's twice as nice to share the prizes!

- Autographed photo of Mary-Kate and Ashley
- A complete library of TWO OF A KIND™, THE NEW ADVENTURES OF MARY-KATE AND ASHLEY™, MARY-KATE AND ASHLEY STARRING IN, SO LITTLE TIME and SWEET 16 book series
- Mary-Kate and Ashley videos
- Mary-Kate and Ashley music CDs
- 3 sets of Mary-Kate and Ashley dolls
- Mary-Kate and Ashley video games
- Mary-Kate and Ashley Fantasy Pack

IT COULD BE YOU!

Mail to: **THE NEW ADVENTURES OF MARY-KATE AND ASHLEY**
BEST FRIENDS PRIZE PACK SWEEPSTAKES
   C/O HarperEntertainment
   Attention: Children's Marketing Department
   10 East 53rd Street, New York, NY 10022

No purchase necessary.

Name: _____

Address: _____

City: _____ State: _____ Zip: _____

Phone: _____ Age: _____

 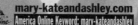

OFFICIAL RULES:

1. No purchase necessary.

2. To enter complete the official entry form or hand print your name, address, age, and phone number along with the words "TH NEW ADVENTURES OF MARY-KATE & ASHLEY Win a Best Friends Prize Pack Sweepstakes" on a 3" x 5" card and mail to: TH NEW ADVENTURES OF MARY-KATE & ASHLEY Win a Best Friends Prize Pack Sweepstakes, c/o HarperEntertainment, Attn: Children's Marketing Department, 10 East 53rd Street, New York, NY 10022. Entries must be received no later than Decemb 31, 2002. Enter as often as you wish, but each entry must be mailed separately. One entry per envelope. Partially complete illegible, or mechanically reproduced entries will not be accepted. Sponsors are not responsible for lost, late, mutilated, illegibl stolen, postage due, incomplete, or misdirected entries. All entries become the property of Dualstar Entertainment Group, Inc., will not be returned.

3. Sweepstakes open to all legal residents of the United States (excluding Colorado and Rhode Island) who are between the age five and fifteen on December 31, 2002, excluding employees and immediate family members of HarperCollins Publishers, Inc ("HarperCollins"), Parachute Properties and Parachute Press, Inc., and their respective subsidiaries and affiliates, officers, direc shareholders, employees, agents, attorneys, and other representatives (individually and collectively "Parachute"), Dualstar Entertainment Group, Inc., and its subsidiaries and affiliates, officers, directors, shareholders, employees, agents, attorneys, an other representatives (individually and collectively "Dualstar"), and their respective parent companies, affiliates, subsidiaries, a tising, promotion and fulfillment agencies, and the persons with whom each of the above are domiciled. Offer void where pro ed or restricted by law.

4. Odds of winning depend on the total number of entries received. Approximately 600,000 sweepstakes announcements publis All prizes will be awarded. Winner will be randomly drawn on or about January 15, 2003, by HarperEntertainment, whose de sions are final. Potential winner will be notified by mail and will be required to sign and return an affidavit of eligibility and re of liability within 14 days of notification. Prizes won by minors will be awarded to parent or legal guardian who must sign an return all required legal documents. By acceptance of prize, winner consents to the use of his or her name, photograph, liken and personal information by HarperCollins, Parachute, Dualstar, and for publicity purposes without further compensation excep where prohibited.

5. One (1) Grand Prize Winner will win a Best Friends Prize Pack to include 2 of each of the following items: autographed phot Mary-Kate and Ashley, THE NEW ADVENTURES OF MARY-KATE & ASHLEY book library, TWO OF A KIND book library, STARRING IN... book library, SO LITTLE TIME book library, SWEET 16 book library; MARY-KATE AND ASHLEY Fantasy Pack; MARY-KATE A ASHLEY GIRLS' NIGHT OUT, CRUSH COURSE, POCKET PLANNER, MAGICAL MYSTERY MALL, WINNERS CIRCLE, and GET A CLUE video games; PASSPORT TO PARIS, BILLBOARD DAD, SWITCHING GOALS, YOU'RE INVITED TO MARY-KATE AND ASHLEY'S GRE EST PARTIES, YOU'RE INVITED TO MARY-KATE AND ASHLEY'S BALLET PARTY, and YOU'RE INVITED TO MARY-KATE AND ASHLEY SCHOOL DANCE PARTY videos; SO LITTLE TIME Mary-Kate doll, SO LITTLE TIME Ashley doll, SWEET 16 doll car, WINNING LON doll giftset; HOLIDAY IN THE SUN, WINNING LONDON, OUR LIPS ARE SEALED, MARY-KATE AND ASHLEY GREATEST HITS, and MARY-KATE AND ASHLEY GREATEST HITS II music CDs. Approximate retail value: $1,500.00.

6. Only one prize will be awarded per individual, family, or household. Prize is non-transferable and cannot be sold or redeemed cash. No cash substitute is available. Any federal, state, or local taxes are the responsibility of the winner. Sponsor may subst prize of equal or greater value, if necessary, due to availability.

7. Additional terms: By participating, entrants agree a) to the official rules and decisions of the judges, which will be final in all respects; and to waive any claim to ambiguity of the official rules and b) to release, discharge, and hold harmless HarperColli Parachute, Dualstar, and their affiliates, subsidiaries, and advertising and promotion agencies from and against any and all lia or damages associated with acceptance, use, or misuse of any prize received in this sweepstakes.

8. Any dispute arising from this Sweepstakes will be determined according to the laws of the State of New York, without referer its conflict of law principles, and the entrants consent to the personal jurisdiction of the State and Federal courts located in Ne York County and agree that such courts have exclusive jurisdiction over all such disputes.

9. To obtain the name of the winner, please send your request and a self-addressed stamped envelope (excluding residents of Vermont and Washington) to THE NEW ADVENTURES OF MARY-KATE & ASHLEY Win a Best Friends Prize Pack Sweepstakes, HarperEntertainment, Attn: Children's Marketing Department, 10 East 53rd Street, New York, NY 10022 by February 1, 200 Sweepstakes Sponsor: HarperCollins Publishers, Inc.

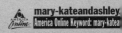

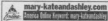

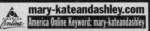